For Sandra and Stephen, with love – A.C.

OXFORD
UNIVERSITY PRESS

Great Clarendon Street, Oxford OX2 6DP

Oxford University Press is a department of the University of Oxford.
It furthers the University's objective of excellence in research, scholarship,
and education by publishing worldwide in

Oxford New York

Auckland Bangkok Buenos Aires Cape Town Chennai
Dar es Salaam Delhi Hong Kong Istanbul Karachi Kolkata
Kuala Lumpur Madrid Melbourne Mexico City Mumbai Nairobi
São Paulo Shanghai Taipei Tokyo Toronto

Oxford is a registered trade mark of Oxford University Press
in the UK and in certain other countries

Text and Illustrations © Anna Currey 2004

The moral rights of the author have been asserted

Database right Oxford University Press (maker)

First published 2004

British Library Cataloguing in Publication Data available

ISBN 0-19-279153-2 Hardback
ISBN 0-19-272534-3 Paperback

1 3 5 7 9 10 8 6 4 2

Printed in China

Jasper's Bath

Written and Illustrated by Anna Currey

OXFORD
UNIVERSITY PRESS

Once there was a rhinoceros called Jasper.
He had everything a rhinoceros could want.
A prickly thorn patch, lots of juicy grass,
and a cool watering hole.

And Jasper wanted to keep
everything all to himself.
So when the birds fluttered
down to drink . . .

. . . Jasper rudely told them to go away.

When the gazelles nibbled
at his prickly thorns,
he glared at them and
stamped his feet.

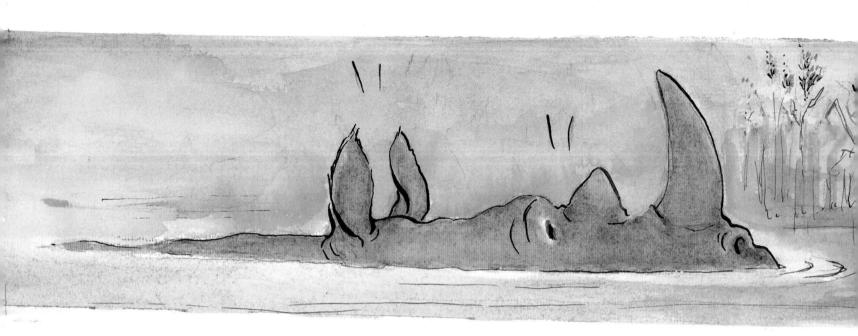

And – oh dear – when Whiskers the rat found him in

. . . well, then Jasper *really* lost his temper. He heaved

his morning bath and asked if he could get in too . . .

himself out of his pool, lowered his head, and *charged.*

He charged
that poor rat
off across
the grass,

past the prickly thorns,

and far out into the bush.

Then he trotted back, feeling very pleased with himself.

But while he was away, who had
been eating his prickly thorns?

Who had been trampling his juicy grass?

And WHO was in his watering hole?

'Hullo,' said the elephant.

'Just having a soak,' he said. 'Won't be long.'
But he was. He was hours and hours.
Soon the birds and the gazelles arrived,
and even Whiskers the rat.

'Can I just paddle my feet at
the edge here?' he asked.

'Nope, sorry, I need that bit,'
the elephant replied.

He tossed and he turned.

He wallowed and he splashed.

He sucked water in,

and he blew
water out,

and he rolled,

and he rolled,

and he rolled.

Jasper didn't know what to do.

'Maybe we could all charge him,' he said at last.

'We could run at him like this,'

and he pawed the ground and frowned horribly.

But the birds hung back, and the
gazelles shook their heads.
Even Whiskers the rat refused.
'No,' he said. 'Being
charged isn't
really
very nice.'

'Oh,' said Jasper. 'Isn't it?'
and he wriggled uncomfortably.

At last, when the sun
was low, the elephant
hauled himself
to his feet.

'Ah well, must be going,'
he said happily.
And he ambled off towards the sunset,
taking most of the pool with him.

The animals sat in the muddy puddle that was left
and watched him go. 'Selfish beast!' snorted Whiskers.
For the first time in his life, Jasper felt rather small.

'I suppose,' he said slowly, looking around, 'I *suppose* that there's plenty of room for everyone. As long as they don't splash too much,' he added quickly.

The watering hole soon filled again, but now,
when the birds fluttered down to drink, and
the gazelles nibbled at the thorn leaves,
Jasper didn't stamp and snort and roar.
He didn't tell them all to go away.

In fact, he was quite pleased to see them.